Curt Schilling

PHILLIE PHIRE!

by
Paul Hagen

SPORTS PUBLISHING INC.
www.SportsPublishingInc.com

Book design, editor: Susan M. McKinney
Cover design: Scot Muncaster
Photos: *The Associated Press*, Rosemary Rahn, Ira Beckoff, and Don Brewer

ISBN: 1-58261-055-x
Library of Congress Catalog Card Number: 99-61953

SPORTS PUBLISHING INC.
SportsPublishingInc.com

Printed in the United States.

Contents

CHAPTER ONE

"What if i Can Never Pitch Again?"

Curt Schilling woke up in the hospital on the morning of August 23, 1995, with an agonizing pain in his right shoulder. Dr. Craig Morgan, who had repaired a torn muscle and removed a bone spur, was standing next to the bed. The surgeon was smiling.

He explained that the procedure had gone well. The rotator cuff wasn't torn. There was no reason the Philadelphia Phillies star shouldn't make a complete recovery.

Curt wasn't so sure. "My shoulder felt like it was on fire," he recalled.

When he went home, he hung a pulley from the wall to begin his rehabilitation. His shoulder hurt so badly he couldn't even lift his arm.

"What if I can never pitch again?" was the thought that kept running through Curt's mind.

He tried not to think about the possibility. He couldn't help himself.

Curt was just 28 years old. Since being traded to the Phillies three years earlier his career had started to come together.

He had been the Opening Day starting pitcher that season for the second consecutive year. He was off to a good start, striking out almost one batter per inning. Then it happened.

Curt's last start had been against the Colorado Rockies in Denver. Everything was normal until the seventh inning when his velocity suddenly dropped

10 miles an hour. There was no pain. He didn't realize anything was wrong at the time.

He woke up the next morning at the team hotel. He noticed that his arm was a little more stiff than usual the day after a game. When he went to take a shower, Curt realized he couldn't raise his arm.

"I was nervous, because I knew that wasn't normal," he said. "But I was trying to be as optimistic as I could be."

When he went to Coors Field that afternoon, he tried to pretend that nothing was wrong. Finally, he approached trainer Jeff Cooper.

Two weeks later, Curt was given the diagnosis he had been dreading. He was told he had a torn rotator cuff.

"Even with modern technology, for a power pitcher, that usually signals the end of something,"

When Curt had surgery on his shoulder in 1995, he was afraid he might never pitch again.

he explained. "That was when I really began to think back and realize that it might all be over."

Curt decided to get a second opinion from Dr. Morgan in Wilmington, Delaware. This time, the news was more encouraging.

The surgery confirmed what Dr. Morgan suspected. The rotator cuff wasn't torn after all.

"It all kind of hit me that day and the next morning when I came home," Curt remembered. "I put up the pulley to raise my arm. That's kind of like walking. It's not something you ever think you'll need to relearn.

"And I couldn't do it. That's when I started thinking there was no way I would ever be able to throw a baseball the way I did before.

"I started to think back to a lot of things I did when I was younger. I used that as a good excuse. I thought, 'I'm just a young kid. I'm learning.' It

wasn't until six or eight months later that I realized how lucky I was to be getting a second chance."

Until then, Curt hadn't been as dedicated as he could have been. Sometimes he worked hard, sometimes he didn't.

"I had never done it consistently," he said. "I'd work myself up. Then I'd kind of slide a little bit until I felt the need to push myself again.

"But I realized it could never, ever be that way again. There's no question that there was not another event that would have made me adjust the way I had to after the surgery."

The injury might have turned out to be the best thing that could have happened to Curt.

Now he fully understood how much baseball meant to him. Now he knew that talent alone wasn't enough.

And when he recovered, he wasn't throwing the ball the way he did before. To nearly everyone's amazement, he was throwing even better.

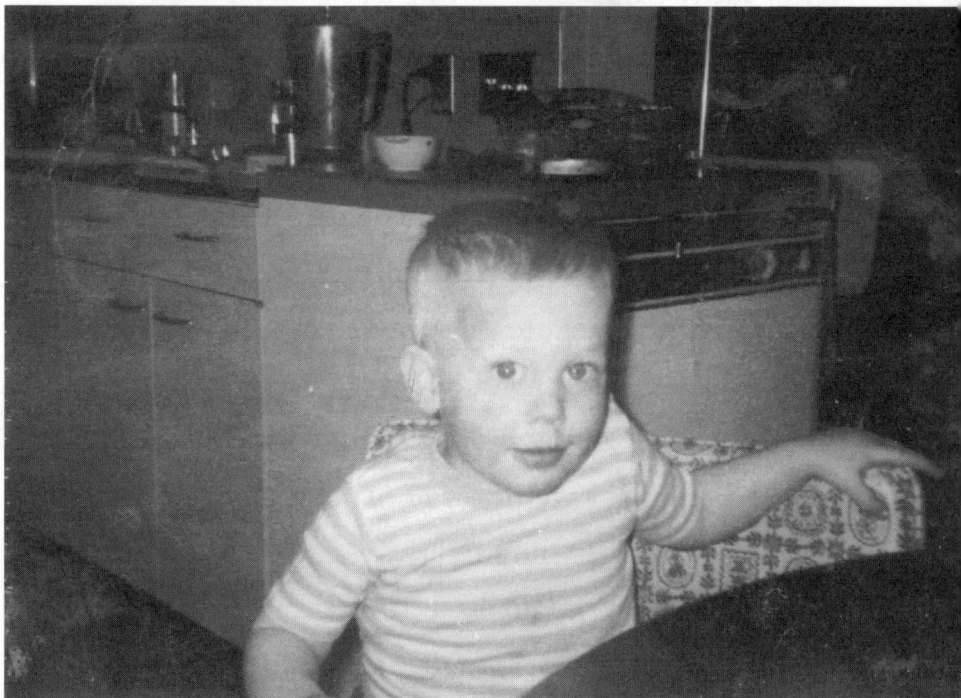

Curt, 1 1/2 years old in this picture, was born in Anchorage, Alaska, while his father was in the Army.

CHAPTER TWO 2

Northern Exposure

Not many future major league All-Stars have been born in Anchorage, Alaska. In fact, Curt is the only one, coming into the world on November 14, 1966.

His father was in the Army, stationed at Elmendorf Air Force Base. From the beginning, it was obvious that sports was going to be a big part of Curt's life.

When his mother brought him home from the hospital, his father had already placed a baseball glove and ball in his crib.

Curt with his dad, Cliff.

The family spent the first two years of Curt's life in Alaska, then moved several times. They lived in Kentucky, Illinois and Missouri.

By the time he was ready to begin school, though, the Schillings had settled in Phoenix, Arizona.

Cliff Schilling was born and raised in the heart of coal-mining country in western Pennsylvania. He was a fan of the Pittsburgh Pirates and Steelers. Those teams became Curt's passion as well.

"A lot of the best memories in my life revolve around my father and the Pirates or my father and the Steelers," he said.

"My father's favorite athletes became mine, too. Roberto Clemente. The first professional game I ever attended was his last game. Double off Jon Matlack for his 3,000th hit. I loved Mean Joe Greene. All the guys my father loved. Because I held my father in such high regard that anybody he talked

Curt (top row, second from left) with his Little League team at the age of 14.

that way about had to be superhuman to me.

"I also liked to watch Nolan Ryan and J.R. Richard. I always liked power pitchers when I was young, anybody with power."

It's not surprising, then, that he took to sports right away. The first video of Curt taken outside his house shows him throwing a Wiffle Ball when he was two.

"I couldn't walk away from anything else and feel the way I felt about competing. And I learned that very young from my father," he said.

Curt participated in several different sports while growing up. The weather in Arizona allowed him to play year round. Still, he always seemed to come back to baseball.

That didn't mean he was always bigger and better than other kids his age, though. In fact, he didn't make the varsity baseball team until he was a senior at Shadow Mountain High School.

Again, however, what appeared to be a setback at the time ended up as a positive experience.

Curt did some pitching in Little League and during the summer, but he usually played third base. He could always throw hard, but he also enjoyed hitting.

"I had a difference of opinion with the varsity coach," Curt said. "It was an unfortunate thing. We just didn't see eye-to-eye. But to this day I have a lot of respect for him.

"I learned a valuable lesson. I learned that no matter what you think is fair in life, sometimes it's not what everybody else sees. Whether it was fair or not that I didn't play varsity until my senior year was beside the point."

That lesson started with what could have been an ugly situation. Some of the more influential families in town began circulating a petition to have the coach fired after their sons didn't make the team.

Curt's father was opposed to the petition. "Because, first, it wasn't right," Curt explained. "Secondly, it was not the way you did things.

"My dad told me, 'You're going to play for men you don't agree with. Some you won't like. Your options are to shut up and play or quit.' The rule I always had was never to speak back to an umpire or a coach."

Curt still stays in touch with those who helped shape his early career. One coach he had in his early teens, Dave Zall, took a special interest. Once he brought a major leaguer out to watch Curt pitch. Frequently, he kept Curt after practice for additional workouts.

"He'd tell me what I was going to have to do if I was going to make it," Curt said. "I was blessed with a lot of tremendous men as coaches, including Mike McQuaid and Walt McConnell, while I was growing up. And I learned a lot. Not just about baseball, but about life."

His dad never managed a team Curt played for. He always volunteered to be an assistant coach instead, close enough to be involved, but never interfering.

After Curt's junior year in high school, he attended a tryout camp held by the Cincinnati Reds. The scouts seemed interested. . .until they learned he hadn't graduated yet.

By now, the varsity coach had noticed newspaper stories about Curt's success on the mound and asked him to pitch as a senior.

Curt wasn't drafted at the end of the season, although he did talk about signing with the Milwaukee Brewers. Those conversations ended when his left elbow was broken after being hit by a pitch in a summer league game. At least he was able to take his first family vacation.

That fall, Curt enrolled at Yavapai Junior College in Arizona. That became a memorable experience as the team advanced to the JUCO World Series.

"We were the No. 1 junior college team in the nation," he said. "Our catcher, Brian Deak, was the Player of the Year and a third-round pick by the Braves that year. It was one of the greatest, most fun years of my life, due in large part to my coach, Dave Dangler."

It was the first time Curt had lived away from home. Yavapai Junior College was about four hours away. His dad could attend all the games, many of which were played in the Phoenix area.

This time, the professional teams took notice.

The Boston Red Sox selected Curt in the second round of the January, 1986, draft. A week later, he signed for $20,000.

He was 19 years old and couldn't wait to take his first steps toward the major leagues.

CHAPTER THREE

Two Steps Forward, One Step Back

There was never any doubt that Curt would quickly sign with the Red Sox.

Ray Boone, the Red Sox scout, made it clear he wasn't going to fool around.

"I'm not going to haggle with you over money," he told Curt. "If it's that big an issue, then you're not the player I want. This is going to be meal money for you someday."

Curt wanted to play so badly that money wasn't an issue. He quickly agreed to the contract and was assigned to Elmira in the Class A New York-Penn League.

On the field, Curt excelled. He went 7-3 and led the team with a 2.59 earned run average.

Off the field, not surprisingly, he reacted the way most youngsters experiencing real freedom for the first time would act.

"I went from Yavapai Junior College to professional baseball," he said. "I expected to be told how to walk, how to talk, how to do everything.

"But it wasn't that way. You had to show up for the workouts and show up for the games. There was a lot of free time. It was a culture shock from that point of view. It was almost like going to school without the classes.

"What a blast. I had so much fun. And got in so much trouble. But I had a good time and a good season."

In 1987, Curt pitched for Greensboro, North Carolina. He led the Class A South Atlantic League in strikeouts with 189 in 184 innings. He also led the league with 15 losses.

"That was the worst team I ever played on in my life," he said.

The biggest loss of his life came after the season, however. His father passed away on January 31, 1988.

"That was tough because the first two years of my career he was the guy I called every week, if not every day, when I needed to," Curt said.

"Now I didn't have that calming voice to tell me everything was all right when I thought it wasn't."

He remembered the first time his father came to see him pitch professionally. Curt had been named to the South Atlantic League All-Star team and had been voted the Player of the Month. His dad accepted the award for him on the field.

"And then I went out and lasted like one and a third innings and gave up eight runs," Curt said. "I was leaving the park and he said, laughingly, 'I didn't come here to see that.' I was incredibly upset because I wanted him to be proud. But I know he was proud of me."

Most of his coaches, former teammates in high school and junior college and kids he grew up with attended his father's wake. Two weeks later, he had to leave for spring training.

He was the last pitcher to make the roster at Double-A New Britain, Connecticut, of the Eastern League, by far the youngest player on the team, and opened the season in the bullpen.

He was inserted into the starting rotation early in the season and was pitching well when he got another shock. On July 30 he was traded along with outfielder Brady Anderson to the Orioles for lefthanded pitcher Mike Boddicker.

A month later, he was in the big leagues.

It had all happened so fast. He had no way of knowing, of course, that it would take four more years and two more trades before he finally began to establish himself as a major leaguer.

CHAPTER FOUR

Up and Down

After the trade, Curt joined Baltimore's Double A team in Charlotte, North Carolina. On the final day of the season, he was called into manager Craig Biagini's office for a telephone call. On the phone was Orioles director of player personnel Doug Melvin.

He congratulated Curt on his season and told him the Orioles wanted him to spend September with the big league team.

The next day, Curt flew to Seattle. As he walked into the Kingdome dugout, the first pitch of the game was thrown by Seattle's Mike Moore. Joe Orsulak hit it for a home run.

Curt warmed up that night. He was so nervous that three of his pitches rolled onto the playing field.

"I was a mess," he said.

Coincidentally, his first major league start came against the Red Sox.

"I remember getting on the mound. Wade Boggs was in the batter's box," he said. "I had left a ticket for my father and I remember thinking that I knew exactly what he would have looked like. He would have been wearing the same thing he always wore: cutoff blue golf shorts and an Orioles tee shirt and cap. And he would have been grinning something fierce."

Curt lasted seven innings that night. His remaining three starts weren't as memorable.

"I got bombed," he said.

Driving home after that turbulent season, Curt felt oddly elated. He realized that he wasn't ready to compete in the big leagues yet, but was quietly confident that he was on the right track.

"I really believed that I was there, that I just had to make some changes and adjustments," he said.

By the time the 1989 season opened, though, Curt had decided he was ready for the big leagues after all. So he was upset when he was sent to Triple-A Rochester, New York. He admits he didn't handle it as well as he should have.

"I kind of let it go," he said. "I just showed up and pitched. Guys were getting called up ahead of me. I would think, 'I'm better than that guy. Why aren't I being called up?' It's the same thing a lot of guys think.

"I was just real immature at the time. I was partying. I was living that life. I was having fun and

I wasn't paying attention to why. I was having fun because baseball was providing me with a lot of things."

Once again, Curt was a September call-up for the Orioles. Once again, he didn't pitch very well.

The start of the 1990 season was delayed by an owners' lockout. While waiting for the labor dispute to be settled, Curt worked out with the Towson State University team. A week before the players were called back to work, he developed tendinitis in his elbow.

Still, he pitched well enough in spring training to convince himself that he had a chance to make the Orioles. He recalls asking one of the beat writers where he fit in.

"You've got no chance," he told Curt. "They haven't even mentioned your name in a meeting.

Sure enough, he was soon told he was going back to Rochester.

*When Schilling reported to the Orioles with long hair
and an earring in 1990, manager Frank Robinson told
him he wouldn't be allowed to pitch until he cut his
hair and took out the earring.*

"I was crushed," Curt said. "I was really upset."

That began to show in his appearance. By the time he was called up on June 29, he had a blue streak dyed into his hair and he was wearing a diamond earring.

This time Curt joined the team at the Metrodome in Minneapolis. Manager Frank Robinson took one look at him and summoned him to the office.

Robinson had his head down when Curt walked in. He looked up briefly, then looked down again. He heaved a deep, disappointed sigh.

Even though Curt had washed the dye from his hair, his hair was still spiked on top and long in the back. And he was still wearing the earring.

Finally, the manager spoke. "What is that?" he said. "You're not going to pitch for me until your hair is cut and that earring is gone."

Curt and his wife, Shonda, met in Baltimore in 1990.
(Photo by Ira Beckoff).

Curt left the office. He immediately took the earring out. Then he went to locate a pair of clippers to trim his hair.

That night he got into the game and earned the first save of his career.

Curt really thought he had become part of that team. He enjoyed many of the younger players like Steve Finley, Mike Devereaux and Pete Harnisch. He loved the city of Baltimore.

Best of all, the day after the season ended, walking in a mall, he met Shonda Brewer. She was then a television personality in Baltimore. He was a rising star.

"We became inseparable from that day forward," he said.

Once again, baseball threw Curt a curve. In early January, 1991 he was eating breakfast when the phone rang. It was Orioles general manager Roland Hemond.

Curt and Shonda on Family Day in 1998 with Gehrig (front left) and Gabriella. (Photo by Rosemary Rahn).

"I just wanted to call and let you know we've made a trade," he said.

Curt didn't catch on right away.

"Great!" he said. "Who did we get?"

Now, Curt shakes his head at how naive he was. "It didn't dawn on me that the general manager wouldn't be calling just to let me know they'd made a trade," he said. "He told me it was Glenn Davis from the Houston Astros and that was the reason he was calling."

When Curt told Shonda, a Baltimore native whose family still lived in the area, she began crying.

"I had really wanted to be a part of that team and that city," Curt said. "So we immediately had a decision to make on our future. Luckily, she decided to stick by my side."

Less than two years later, they were married. Now they have two children, Gehrig Clifford and Gabriella Patricia.

Photo by: Rosemary Rahn.

Gehrig, Curt, Shonda and Gabriella, Christmas, 1998.

Being traded to Houston wasn't the only change in Curt's career that year. Until then, he had been used mostly as a starter. But when he was asked in a conference call with the Houston media what role he preferred, he said he'd like to try being a closer.

"There was a lot of money to be made there," he explained. "Guys get famous closing."

Curt reported to Houston's training site in Kissimmee, Florida. He had a good spring and opened the 1991 season as the Astros closer. Even though the Astros were losing, the atmosphere in the clubhouse was good. Again, he began to feel a part of the team.

Six weeks later he was in Triple-A Tucson, Arizona.

"I couldn't get Shonda out," he said. "I was really at an emotional crossroads. I had no idea what was going on. I was just pitching horribly."

Slowly, he began to find himself again. He returned to the majors when the Astros traded Jim Clancy to the Atlanta Braves.

"I remember thinking, 'All right, this is how the story goes in the movies,'" he said. "I thought everything was going to turn around. And I went out that first night and walked four straight batters."

That wasn't the most embarrassing thing that happened that night, either. After he left the game, Curt went into the tunnel under the stands and began beating the railing with a bat, using every bad word that he could think of.

When he came out of the clubhouse later that night, Shonda and her mother were waiting. They stared at him, wide-eyed. They had heard every word of his tirade.

Curt pitched decently for the rest of the season. That winter, a chance encounter in the Astrodome weight room left a lasting impression.

Roger Clemens, who was also working out that day, sent word that he'd like to talk to Curt.

"He called me over and he proceeded to chew me out," Curt said. "He berated me for a lack of integrity and a lack of discipline. And everything he said hit the nail right on the head.

"The one thought I walked away with was that here was a guy with all those Cy Young Awards and he's going to take two hours out of his precious workout time to talk to me. And not just talk, but do it with a lot of intensity. It was not just lip service.

"I took it to heart. It still took me time to develop the habits I needed. But I certainly looked differently then at the way things worked."

Before Curt was able to really put his latest lesson to use, though, he found himself traded again.

CHAPTER FIVE

The Philadelphia Story

Major league teams were breaking camp across Florida and Arizona on April 2, 1992 when Curt was told that he had been traded again. This time he was going to the Phillies for righthander Jason Grimsley.

Shaken, he looked up at a beat writer standing near his locker. "They keep telling me what a great arm I have. So why do I keep getting traded?" he asked.

Actually, the reason was simple. Curt was out of options. That meant the Astros couldn't send him

Curt was traded to the Phillies in April, 1992.

back to the minors without putting him on waivers, where he would certainly have been claimed. All Houston would have gotten in return was $25,000.

Management didn't think they could keep him in the big leagues, either, because he had pitched poorly that spring. So general manager Bob Watson, under the gun, made what he believed was the best deal available.

The Phillies were scheduled to play their final exhibition game against the Pittsburgh Pirates at Joe Robbie Stadium in Miami.

A steady drizzle forced the cancellation of the game. But Curt was able to throw in the bullpen for Phillies manager Jim Fregosi and pitching coach Johnny Podres that afternoon.

Both men were impressed. "He's got the arm of a starter," Fregosi said to Podres, who nodded in vigorous agreement.

Curt noticed a different attitude almost from the moment he joined the Phillies.

"I was a little bit confused after the Astros traded me, but I was obviously blind to the fact that I still wasn't putting the effort in," he said.

"They said some things when I left, some personal stuff, that I wasn't happy with. Bob Watson bad-mouthed me a little bit because of my work habits. At the time, I was really upset. My first thought was that I was going to show those guys.

"Looking back on it, though, the things I wasn't happy with were probably true. I wasn't having any fun in Houston, but most of that was my fault. Had I been a good pitcher then, they wouldn't have traded me."

The Phillies, by contrast, were encouraging from the beginning. Podres oohed and ahed all the way through that first bullpen session and told Curt to stay ready, that he would be a starter for the Phillies before long.

"It was the first time in a long time I'd walked off the mound feeling that good about myself," he said. "It was really positive and I needed that badly."

For the next two months, Curt worked harder than he had in a long time.

He got his first Phillies start on May 19, 1992, and, to make the story even better, it came against the Astros. He pitched six shutout innings and the Phillies won.

His season got even better. When the year ended he had held opponents to a .201 batting average, lowest in the league, and was among the leaders in earned run average (2.35), complete games (10) and shutouts (four).

The best was yet to come.

Curt and other Phillies pitchers work out during spring training in 1996.

CHAPTER SIX

That Championship Season

The Phillies finished last in the National League East in 1992 but you never would have known it by the time the players gathered at the Carpenter Complex in Clearwater, Florida, the following spring.

"Two or three days in, we all knew it was something pretty special," Curt said. "We all felt from the get-go that we were the team to beat."

The Phillies opened the 1993 season in Houston against an Astros team that had made a splash

in the offseason by signing free agents Doug Drabek and Greg Swindell. Many picked Houston to win the National League West, but the Phillies swept the Astros in the Dome and never looked back.

"I remember flying home after that series and thinking, wow, that was pretty impressive," Curt said.

The Phillies went from worst to first, winning 97 games. Curt was a big part of that, going 16-7. Still, when the National League Championship Series opened at Veterans Stadium, the Phillies were decided underdogs.

Curt was named the Phillies starter for the play-off opener and that meant a lot to him.

"I desperately wanted to be the No. 1 guy on that staff," he said. "Terry Mulholland was the staff ace, but that was the job I wanted from day one."

Curt has always had the ability to rise to the occasion and the determination to be the No. 1

starter was just a part of that. He enjoys pressure and expectations. It makes him perform better. And October 6, 1993 was no exception.

"I went to bed the night before and I was unbelievably nervous," he said. "But I fell asleep right away and woke up the next morning feeling great. I told myself I didn't want the adrenaline to be bad. For some reason, when I pitch, I can always channel it perfectly.

"While I was warming up, I could feel all that energy at the Vet. Walking to the mound was like nothing I'd ever experienced before."

Curt settled down quickly, striking out the first five Braves batters he faced. He ended up pitching eight innings and allowing two runs on seven hits but didn't get a decision as the Phillies won in 10 innings.

His second start came in Game 5 at Atlanta-Fulton County Stadium. This time he allowed one earned run in eight-plus innings. Again, the Phillies won in extra innings.

The team wrapped up the pennant in six games. Curt was named the Most Valuable Player of the NLCS. Then it was time to move on to play the defending world champion Toronto Blue Jays in the World Series.

"That was fun, but it was more of a show," Curt said. "If you don't win in the playoffs, you haven't really done anything. When you go to the World Series, you're the champion of a league.

"I didn't see how anybody could beat us. Only something screwy could keep us from winning."

Curt was the losing pitcher in Game 1 but came back to pitch a five-hit shutout that kept the Phillies alive in Game 5.

The Phillies led into the bottom of the ninth of Game 6. Curt was already thinking ahead to the decisive seventh game when Joe Carter ended it with a dramatic three-run homer at SkyDome.

"As the ball was going out, my first thought was that I had just witnessed one of the greatest moments in baseball history," Curt said. "I had chills for an hour. It didn't hit me for a good five minutes that it was over. It was done. But it didn't seem right. It didn't fit. And it stunk, because we had to go home."

In the clubhouse, an emotional manager Jim Fregosi told the media that there could never be such a magical season again.

It didn't take long for Fregosi to be proven right.

CHAPTER SEVEN

The Fall and the Redemption

If 1993 was a dream season, 1994 quickly turned into a nightmare for the Phillies.

And as much as Curt was a part of the team's success a year earlier, he had a role in the collapse the following season.

By now he had reached his goal of becoming the team's undisputed No. 1 pitcher, earning the Opening Day assignment for the first time in his career.

After nine starts, he was 0-7, the longest losing streak of his career. For the first time, he was experiencing serious physical problems.

He left one game after four innings with a sprained ligament in his foot. A month later, he went on the disabled list for the first time in his career with a tender right elbow that required surgery to remove a bone spur.

He returned to action just in time to suffer a freak injury when his left knee popped as he got out of a chair. Another operation was necessary.

That was nothing compared to what was ahead for Curt in 1995.

He got off to a strong start, winning his first four decisions. He was among the National League leaders in innings pitched, strikeouts and opponent's batting average when he began experiencing the shoulder problems that eventually landed him on Dr. Morgan's operating table.

That's when it all came together for Curt. His father's reminder that life isn't always fair. His sometimes lackadaisical approach in the minors. The words of Frank Robinson and Roger Clemens and Bob Watson came back to him. He remembered all the times he promised himself to work harder but didn't follow through.

"Most of it was mental," he said. "It was how I looked at things. I'm a procrastinator. I'm one of the laziest people you'll ever meet. I love to sleep. I always have.

"But when this happened, it made me stop and think about how I want to be remembered when I'm done. And I realized that it's too late to make the Hall of Fame, but that I'd like to be thought of as one of the best pitchers of my era.

"People who watched baseball in the late 1990s and hopefully for the next five or six or seven years, I want them to say I was one of the best they ever saw.

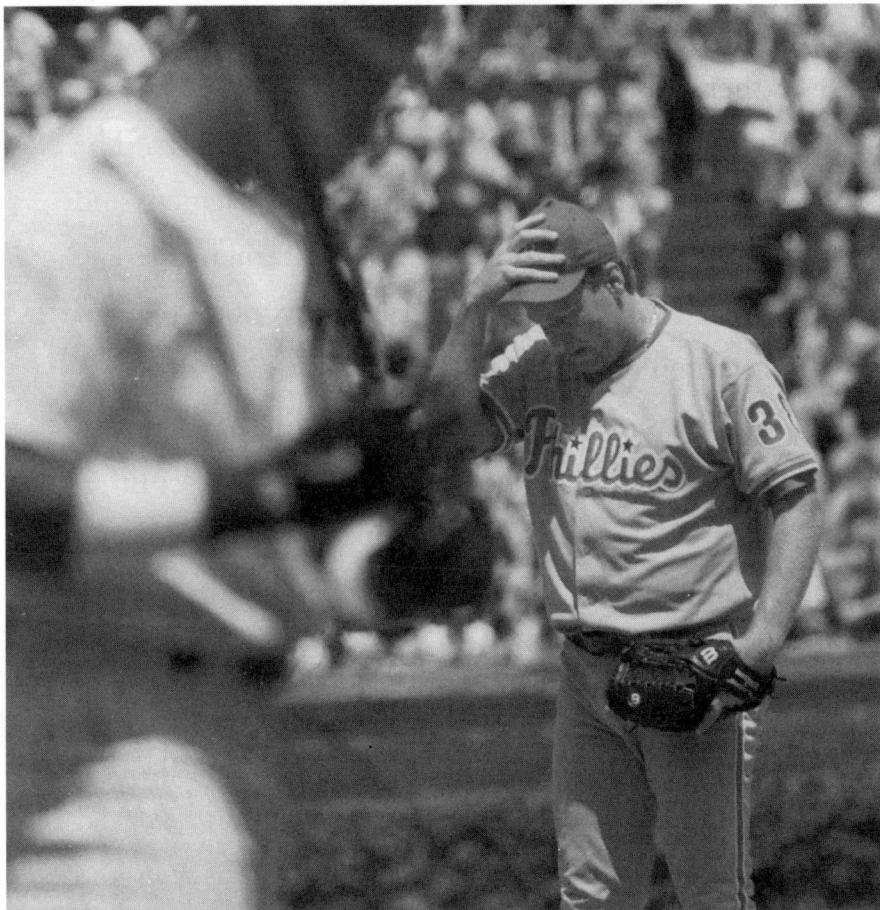

After his surgery in 1995, Curt changed his approach to pitching.

"And there's only one way to get there. That's by maxing out, doing everything you can. Conditioning, scouting, mental preparation. Whatever has to be done, you've got to do it.

"I sort of changed my tune a little bit. I only have to look back at that period and realize I'm only cheating myself if I don't get it done."

Curt built a weight room in the basement of his house. Instead of adding to his written scouting reports on hitters every once in awhile he began keeping a video library and updating it religiously after every start.

He developed a routine in which he goes over his upcoming opponent with coach John Vukovich the day before his start, then reviews the material with his catcher a few hours before he takes the mound.

The results began to show when he returned from the disabled list in May, 1996. Despite miss-

Curt with his son, Gehrig, 3, at the 1998 All-Star Game.

ing the first month-and-a-half of the season, he led the National League with eight complete games.

It was in 1997, though, that Curt caught the attention of baseball fans around the country. He not only made the All-Star team for the first time, but by midseason it was apparent that he had a chance to become just the 13th pitcher this century to strike out 300 batters in a season.

He did that and more. When Edgardo Alfonzo of the Mets became his 300th victim on September 16, Curt had reached the milestone in just 236⅔ innings, the quickest of any pitcher in history.

He ended the season with 319 strikeouts, more than any NL righthander in history, breaking Steve Carlton's Phillies record along the way.

"I didn't really allow myself to think I had a chance at 300 until I got to 299," Curt said. "People may laugh at that but I've learned that you can never, ever, ever, ever take anything for granted.

NL ALL-STARS PITCHERS

ASHBY

BROWN

GLAVINE

HOFFMAN

MADDUX

NEN

REED

SCHILLING

SHAW

URBINA

"So many things can happen. You can get hit with a line drive that ends your season.

"But I knew it was something I wanted by the middle of the year when I realized I was on a pace to do it if I stayed healthy."

Coming into the 1998 season, though, Curt found himself doubting himself.

"I was just afraid that (319 strikeouts) was an aberration, that I'd caught lightning in a bottle," he said. "Because I'd never thrown that way before."

When Curt arrived in Clearwater for spring training, though, he found that at age 31 he felt better than ever.

The hard work, the lessons learned, continued to pay off. He became just the fifth pitcher in history to strike out 300 batters in back-to-back seasons and made his second consecutive All-Star team.

He did that even though his split-fingered fastball deserted him for much of the season. He had 15 complete games. The only disappointment was his 15-14 record, partly because the Phillies scored three or fewer runs in 22 of his 35 starts.

"I persevered," Curt said with a shrug. "And I'm still healthy. So I learned another big lesson."

Epilogue

Curt entered the 1999 season with an opportunity to join his onetime hero, Nolan Ryan, as the only pitchers in history to strike out at least 300 batters three years in a row.

"Am I lucky enough to have this happen to me?" he asked. "Not to strike out 300, but to be healthy and play another baseball season. It's not right that I get to have this much fun six months every year."

Curt has always had a profound interest in World War II, small unit tactics, and the personalities that arise during a time of war. He said, "Advanced Squad Leader was my game of choice as a kid because I could learn about history right from

Curt has a chance to become only the second pitcher to strike out at least 300 batters three years in a row.

the box. Being an avid board gamer, an Avalon Hill wargamer, has opened a lot of doors for me and allowed me to meet people and go places I might not have been able to do otherwise. John Wayne, The Dirty Dozen, The Rat Patrol were all staples of my childhood and my interests away from the game of baseball."

One of Curt's joys is that he has been able to form his own company, along with his close friends Brian Youse, Perry Cocke, Russ Bunten, Carl Fago, Steve Petersen, and Chuck Goetz, called Multi-Man Publishing. And now, in partnership with Hasbro Games they produce and sell the entire Advanced Squad Leader Gaming System.

Curt's life isn't all fun and games, though. The enjoyment comes from the results. The results come from hard work, the kind that has allowed Curt to have his best years after he turned 30.

"My only goal since I've gotten hurt is to walk away healthy at the end of the season," he said.

"Because I honestly believe, with the kind of pitcher I am, then I'll have the numbers at the end of the year.

It may have taken Curt a few years to learn all his lessons. Obviously, however, he has learned them well.

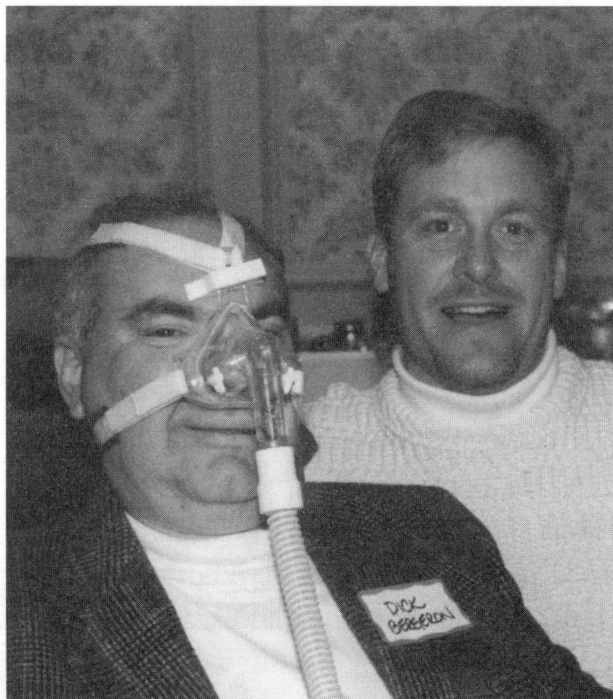

Curt with ALS patient Dick Bergeron, who inspired Curt and Shonda to become involved with ALS (Lou Gehrig's disease). The Schillings have raised over $1 million for ALS research and patient care. (photo: Ira Beckoff)

Curt Schilling Quick Facts

Full Name: Curtis Montague Schilling
Team: Philadelphia Phillies
Hometown: Anchorage, Alaska
Position: Pitcher
Jersey Number: 38
Bats: Right
Throws: Right
Height: 6-4
Weight: 225 pounds
Birthdate: November 14, 1966

1998 Highlights: Led the National League in strikeouts (300) and led the majors in complete games (15) and innings pitched (268.2)

Stats Spotlight: Became just the fifth pitcher in Major League Baseball history to strike out 300 batters in back-to-back seasons

Little known fact: Schilling personally donates $1,000 per win and $100 per strikeout to Curt's Pitch for ALS (Lou Gehrig's Disease), a total of $45,000 in 1998.

Curt Schilling's Professional Career

Year	Club	W-L	ERA	G	GS	CG	SHO	SV	IP	H	R	ER	BB	SO
1986	Elmira	7-3	2.59	16	15	2	1	0	93.2	92	34	27	30	75
1987	Greensboro	8-15*	3.82	29	28	7	3	0	184.0	179	96	78	65	189*
1988	New Britain	8-5	2.97	21	17	4	1	0	106.0	91	44	35	40	62
	Charlotte	5-2	3.18	7	7	2	1	0	45.1	36	19	16	23	32
	Baltimore	0-3	9.82	4	4	0	0	0	14.2	22	19	16	10	4
1989	Rochester	#13-11	3.21	27	27#	9#	3#	0	185.1	*176	76	66	59	109
	Baltimore	0-1	6.28	5	1	0	0	0	8.2	10	6	6	3	6
1990	Rochester	4-4	3.92	15	14	1	0	0	87.0	95	46	38	25	83
	Baltimore	1-2	2.54	35	0	0	0	3	46.0	38	13	13	19	32
1991	Tucson	0-1	3.42	13	0	0	0	3	23.2	16	9	9	12	21
	Houston	3-5	3.81	56	0	0	0	8	75.2	79	35	32	39	71
1992	Phillies	14-11	2.35	42	26	10	4	2	226.1	165	67	59	59	147
1993	Phillies	16-7	4.02	34	34	7	2	0	235.1	234	114	105	57	186
1994	Phillies	2-8	4.48	13	13	1	0	0	82.1	87	42	41	28	58
	Scranton	0-0	1.80	2	2	0	0	0	10.0	6	2	2	5	6
	Reading	0-0	0.00	1	1	0	0	0	4.0	6	0	0	1	4
1995	Phillies	7-5	3.57	17	17	1	0	0	116.0	96	52	46	26	114
1996	Clearwater	2-0	1.29	2	2	0	0	0	14.0	9	2	2	1	17
	Scranton	1-0	1.38	2	2	0	0	0	13.0	9	2	2	5	10
	Phillies	9-10	3.19	26	26	8*	2	0	183.1	149	69	65	50	182
1997	Phillies	17-11	2.97	35	35#	7	2	0	254.1	208	96	84	58	319*
1998	Phillies	15-14	3.25	35	35*	15*	2	0	268.2*	236	101	97	61	300*
Major League Totals		84-77	3.36	302	191	49	12	13	1511.1	1324	614	564	410	1419

*League Leader   #Tied for League Lead

Career Transactions

— Selected by Boston Red Sox in 2nd round of January, 1986, Draft

— Traded to Baltimore Orioles with Brady Anderson (of), July 30, 1988, for Mike Boddicker (rhp)

— Traded to Houston Astros with Pete Harnisch (rhp) and Steve Finley (of), January 10, 1991, for Glenn Davis

— Traded to Philadelphia, April 2, 1992, for Jason Grimsley (rhp)

League Championship Series Statistics

Year	Club, Opp	W-L	ERA	G	GS	CG	SHO	SV	IP	H	R	ER	BB	SO
1993	Phi, Atl	0-0	1.69	2	2	0	0	0	16.0	11	4	3	5	19

World Series Record

Year	Club, Opp	W-L	ERA	G	GS	CG	SHO	SV	IP	H	R	ER	BB	SO
1993	Phi, Tor	1-1	3.52	2	2	1	1	0	15.1	13	7	6	5	9

1998 National League Pitchers Innings Pitched

Curt Schilling	**268.2**
Kevin Brown	257.0
Greg Maddux	251.0
Carlos Perez	241.0
Livan Hernandez	234.1

1998 National League Pitchers Strikeouts

Curt Schilling	**300**
Kevin Brown	257
Kerry Wood	233
Shane Reynolds	209
Greg Maddux	204

1998 National League Pitchers Complete Games

Curt Schilling	**15**
Greg Maddux	9
Livan Hernandez	9
Kevin Brown	7
Carlos Perez	7

Curt Schilling's 1998 Game-by-Game Performance

Date	Opp	W	L	CG	IP	H	R	ER	HR	BB	SO
3/31/98	@NYN	0	0	0	8.0	2	0	0	0	1	9
4/05/98	@Atl	1	0	1	9.0	5	1	1	1	1	15
4/10/98	ATL	1	0	1	9.0	2	0	0	0	1	10
4/15/98	@Fla	0	1	0	7.0	4	3	3	2	6	7
4/21/98	CIN	0	1	0	7.0	7	3	3	0	1	11
4/26/98	StL	1	0	0	8.0	8	3	3	1	2	13
5/02/98	HOU	0	1	0	7.0	5	2	1	0	1	13
5/07/98	ARI	1	0	0	7.0	3	1	1	0	3	12
5/12/98	@LA	1	0	0	7.0	9	3	3	1	1	6
5/17/98	@SD	0	1	1	8.0	7	3	2	1	1	10
5/23/98	@Mon	0	1	1	8.2	5	3	2	0	2	11
5/28/98	@ChN	0	0	0	5.0	10	7	7	1	3	2
6/02/98	MON	0	1	1	9.0	10	4	4	0	2	6

Date	Opp	W	L	CG	IP	H	R	ER	HR	BB	SO
6/07/98	@Tor	0	1	1	8.0	9	3	3	0	2	9
6/12/98	ChN	1	0	0	7.0	4	0	0	0	2	13
6/17/98	PIT	1	0	1	9.0	2	1	1	1	1	10
6/22/98	@Bos	0	0	0	7.0	12	8	8	2	0	10
6/27/98	TB	0	1	0	7.1	13	5	5	1	1	8
7/03/98	MIL	1	0	0	7.0	5	0	0	0	3	5
7/10/98	@Pit	1	0	1	9.0	9	6	6	2	1	5
7/15/98	@Mil	0	1	1	8.0	8	3	3	0	0	4
7/20/98	@Mon	1	0	1	9.0	5	1	1	1	1	9
7/25/98	FLA	0	1	0	7.2	8	5	5	1	2	11
7/31/98	SF	0	0	0	6.0	9	5	5	1	1	5
8/05/98	@SD	0	1	0	6.0	8	4	4	0	4	7
8/10/98	@Ari	1	0	1	9.0	3	0	0	0	1	5
8/15/98	@Col	0	0	0	6.0	11	3	3	0	1	7
8/20/98	ARI	1	0	1	9.0	4	1	1	0	2	14

Date	Opp	W	L	CG	IP	H	R	ER	HR	BB	SO
8/25/98	SD	0	1	0	7.0	6	4	4	1	4	6
8/30/98	@SF	1	0	1	9.0	7	4	4	2	2	5
9/04/98	@Mil	1	0	0	7.0	6	2	2	1	2	10
9/09/98	NYN	0	1	0	6.0	10	3	3	0	2	4
9/14/98	@Atl	0	1	1	8.0	7	4	3	2	2	12
9/19/98	MON	1	0	1	9.0	5	3	3	1	2	9
9/26/98	@Fla	0	0	0	8.0	8	3	3	0	0	7
Totals		**15**	**14**	**15**	**268.2**	**236**	**101**	**97**	**23**	**61**	**300**

ERA: 3.25

Curt Schilling's 1998 Highlights

- Curt "owned" the Arizona Diamondbacks in 1998, posting a perfect 3-0 win-loss record. Through 25 innings pitched against Arizona, he yielded only two earned runs, an ERA of 0.72. Curt gave up just 10 hits in three games and struck out 31 Diamondbacks.

- In multiple appearances against Atlanta and the New York Mets, Curt also had ERAs of less than 2.00. In three games versus the Braves, Curt posted a 1.38 ERA and had 37 strikeouts in 26 innings. In two appearances against the Mets, Curt had a 1.93 ERA, allowing only three earned runs in 14 innings pitched.

- In 1,000 total at-bats, opponent batters hit just .236 against Curt, including .223 by right-handed hitters. When Curt had two strikes on a hitter, those batters hit just .155 against him.

- Curt was especially effective against opponent hitters in night games, registering 205 of his 300 total strikeouts.

- Curt had 15 double-digit strikeout games in 1998. That boosted his career total of 44, tying him with Mark Langston for fifth place among all active pitchers.

Curt Schilling's 1997 Game-by-Game Performance

Date	Opp	W	L	CG	IP	H	R	ER	HR	BB	SO
4/01/97	@LA	1	0	0	8.0	2	0	0	0	3	11
4/06/97	@SD	1	0	0	8.0	7	2	1	1	0	7
4/11/97	SD	0	1	0	6.2	10	7	7	0	2	5
4/16/97	SF	0	0	0	7.0	7	2	2	2	2	6
4/21/97	@Pit	1	0	1	9.0	9	2	2	0	0	8
4/26/97	@Cin	0	1	0	4.0	6	6	6	3	4	3
5/01/97	LA	0	1	0	7.0	3	4	4	1	1	9
5/06/97	@Hou	1	0	0	7.0	7	1	1	0	2	7
5/11/97	COL	1	0	1	9.0	4	1	1	0	0	12
5/17/97	HOU	1	0	0	8.0	3	2	2	1	3	11

Date	Opp	W	L	CG	IP	H	R	ER	HR	BB	SO
5/22/97	NYN	0	1	0	2.2	8	9	1	1	3	3
5/27/97	@Cin	1	0	1	9.0	7	1	1	0	1	11
6/03/97	CIN	0	1	0	6.0	5	3	3	0	4	7
6/08/97	@Pit	1	0	0	8.0	5	2	2	1	2	11
6/13/97	TOR	0	0	0	6.0	6	2	2	0	1	8
6/18/97	@Bos	0	1	0	7.0	7	4	4	0	3	7
6/23/97	FLA	1	0	0	7.0	6	3	2	1	1	13
6/28/97	@Atl	0	1	0	5.2	8	7	7	4	4	12
7/03/97	ChN	0	1	0	8.0	9	5	5	0	1	8
7/11/97	@Fla	1	0	0	6.0	6	2	1	0	3	10
7/16/97	MON	1	0	1	9.0	4	0	0	0	0	7
7/21/97	PIT	0	1	0	8.0	6	3	3	2	1	15
7/26/97	@LA	0	1	0	7.0	7	4	4	3	0	10
7/31/97	StL	0	0	0	9.0	4	1	1	0	3	11
8/05/97	COL	0	0	0	6.0	5	0	0	0	2	12

Date	Opp	W	L	CG	IP	H	R	ER	HR	BB	SO
8/10/97	@StL	1	0	1	9.0	3	0	0	0	1	8
8/15/97	@Hou	1	0	0	8.0	5	1	1	0	1	10
8/22/97	LA	0	0	0	8.1	6	3	3	0	2	12
8/27/97	SD	0	0	0	6.0	6	3	2	1	2	10
9/01/97	NYA	1	0	0	8.0	7	1	1	0	0	16
9/06/97	@Mon	1	0	1	9.0	8	3	3	0	1	10
9/11/97	SF	0	0	0	7.0	6	1	1	0	3	6
9/16/97	NYN	1	0	1	9.0	3	2	2	1	0	9
9/21/97	@ChN	0	1	0	5.0	10	6	6	3	1	8
9/26/97	FLA	1	0	0	7.0	3	3	3	0	1	6
Totals		**17**	**11**	**7**	**254.1**	**208**	**96**	**84**	**25**	**58**	**319**

ERA: 2.97

Curt Schilling—
A Hero Both On and Off the Field

Curt Schilling became involved in the ALS cause in 1992 during his first season with the Phillies. ALS is also known as Lou Gehrig's Disease because it took the life of Lou Gehrig, the "Iron Man of Baseball," in 1941. Curt's dedication to the cause is so great that he and his wife, Shonda, named their first child Gehrig as a tribute to all the ALS patients they had met.

ALS can affect anyone—but usually people between the ages of 30 and 75. Symptoms include the wasting and paralysis of the muscles. It is always fatal and there is no cure. The ALS Association is the one place patients and families can turn for ALS support, care, and programs. The Association also supports cutting-edge research to find a cure for this devastating disease.

The Schillings are wonderful volunteers for the Greater Philadelphia Chapter of the ALS Association. Curt created "Curt's Pitch for ALS" in 1992. He personally donates a minimum of $25,000 based on his wins and strikeouts each season. In 1994, Curt established the "Curt Schilling Golf Outing for ALS." Together, these two programs have raised more than $1 million. The Schillings also attend many other ALS events and Shonda is a very active member of the Chapter Board.

Thanks to the generosity of people like Curt Schilling, there is hope that a cure for ALS will soon be found.

For more information about the ALS Association, or to join "Curt's Pitch for ALS", please call 215-643-5434; FAX 215-643-9307; or visit our website at www.als-phila.org.

The Greater Philadelphia Chapter, ALS Association is proud to be the official charity of the Phillies.

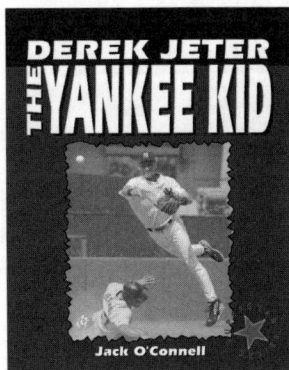

Derek Jeter: The Yankee Kid

Author: Jack O'Connell
ISBN: 1-58261-043-6

In 1996 Derek burst onto the scene as one of the most promising young shortstops to hit the big leagues in a long time. His hitting prowess and ability to turn the double play have definitely fulfilled the early predictions of greatness.

A native of Kalamazoo, MI, Jeter has remained well grounded. He patiently signs autographs and takes time to talk to the young fans who will be eager to read more about him in this book.

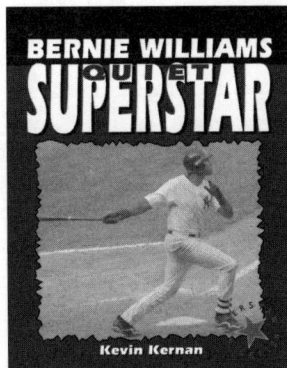

Bernie Williams: Quiet Superstar

Author: Kevin Kernan
ISBN: 1-58261-044-4

Bernie Williams, a guitar-strumming native of Puerto Rico, is not only popular with his teammates, but is considered by top team officials to be the heir to DiMaggio and Mantle fame.

He draws frequent comparisons to Roberto Clemente, perhaps the greatest player ever from Puerto Rico. Like Clemente, Williams is humble, unassuming, and carries himself with quiet dignity. Also like Clemente, he plays with rare determination and a special elegance. He's married, and serves as a role model not only for his three children, but for his young fans here and in Puerto Rico.

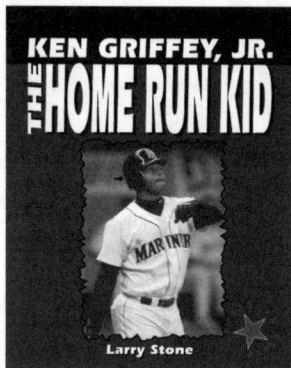

Ken Griffey, Jr.: The Home Run Kid
Author: Larry Stone
ISBN: 1-58261-041-x

Capable of hitting majestic home runs, making breathtaking catches, and speeding around the bases to beat the tag by a split second, Ken Griffey, Jr. is baseball's Michael Jordan. Amazingly, Ken reached the Major Leagues at age 19, made his first All-Star team at 20, and produced his first 100 RBI season at 21.

The son of Ken Griffey, Sr., Ken is part of the only father-son combination to play in the same outfield together in the same game, and, like Barry Bonds, he's a famous son who turned out to be a better player than his father.

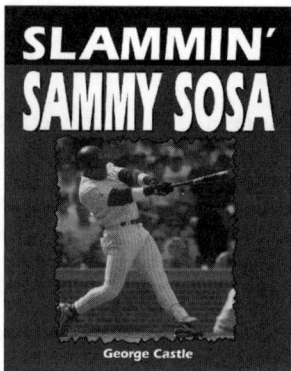

Sammy Sosa: Slammin' Sammy
Author: George Castle
ISBN: 1-58261-029-0

1998 was a break-out year for Sammy as he amassed 66 home runs, led the Chicago Cubs into the playoffs and finished the year with baseball's ultimate individual honor, MVP.

When the national spotlight was shone on Sammy during his home run chase with Mark McGwire, America got to see what a special person he is. His infectious good humor and kind heart have made him a role model across the country.

Mark Grace: Winning with Grace

Author: Barry Rozner
ISBN: 1-58261-056-8

This southern California native and San Diego State alumnus has been playing baseball in the windy city for nearly fifteen years. Apparently the cold hasn't affected his game. Mark is an all-around player who can hit to all fields and play great defense.

Mark's outgoing personality has allowed him to evolve into one of Chicago's favorite sons. He is also community minded and some of his favorite charities include the Leukemia Society of America and Easter Seals.

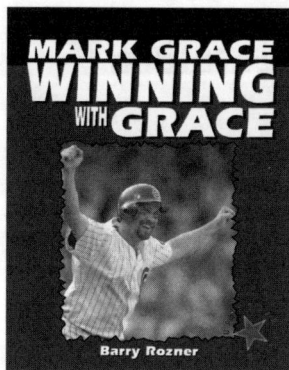

Randy Johnson: Arizona Heat!

Author: Larry Stone
ISBN: 1-58261-042-8

One of the hardest throwing pitchers in the Major Leagues, and, at 6'10" the tallest, the towering figure of Randy Johnson on the mound is an imposing sight which strikes fear into the hearts of even the most determined opposing batters.

Perhaps the most amazing thing about Randy is his consistency in recording strikeouts. He is one of only four pitchers to lead the league in strikeouts for four consecutive seasons. With his recent signing with the Diamondbacks, his career has been rejuvenated and he shows no signs of slowing down.

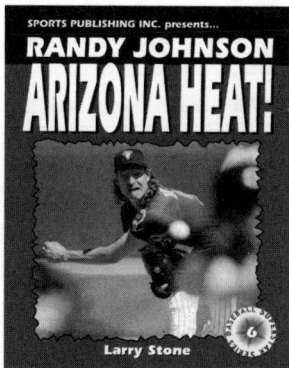

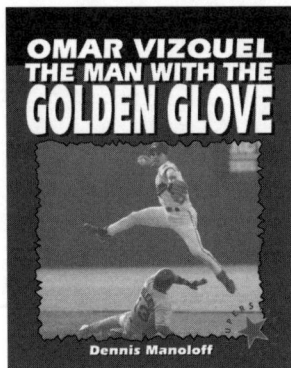

Omar Vizquel: The Man with the Golden Glove

Author: Dennis Manoloff
ISBN: 1-58261-045-2

Omar has a career fielding percentage of .982 which is the highest career fielding percentage for any shortstop with at least 1,000 games played.

Omar is a long way from his hometown of Caracas, Venezuela, but his talents as a shortstop put him at an even greater distance from his peers while he is on the field.

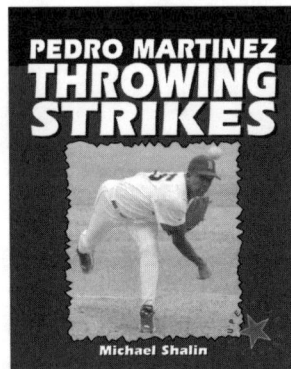

Pedro Martinez: Throwing Strikes

Author: Mike Shalin
ISBN: 1-58261-047-9

The 1997 National League Cy Young Award winner is always teased because of his boyish looks. He's sometimes mistaken for the batboy, but his curve ball and slider leave little doubt that he's one of the premier pitchers in the American League.

It is fitting that Martinez is pitching in Boston, where the passion for baseball runs as high as it does in his native Dominican Republic.

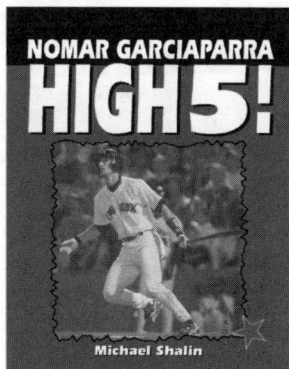

Nomar Garciaparra: High 5!
Author: Mike Shalin
ISBN: 1-58261-053-3

An All-American at Georgia Tech, a star on the 1992 U.S. Olympic Team, the twelfth overall pick in the 1994 draft, and the 1997 American League Rookie of the Year, Garciaparra has exemplified excellence on every level.

At shortstop, he'll glide deep into the hole, stab a sharply hit grounder, then throw out an opponent on the run. At the plate, he'll uncoil his body and deliver a clutch double or game-winning homer. Nomar is one of the game's most complete players.

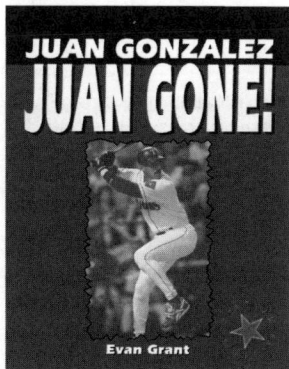

Juan Gonzalez: Juan Gone!
Author: Evan Grant
ISBN: 1-58261-048-7

One of the most prodigious and feared sluggers in the major leagues, Gonzalez was a two-time home run king by the time he was 24 years old.

After having something of a personal crisis in 1996, the Puerto Rican redirected his priorities and now says baseball is the third most important thing in his life after God and family.

Mo Vaughn:
Angel on a Mission

Author: Mike Shalin
ISBN: 1-58261-046-0

Growing up in Connecticut, this Angels slugger learned the difference between right and wrong and the value of honesty and integrity from his parents early on, lessons that have stayed with him his whole life.

This former American League MVP was so active in Boston charities and youth programs that he quickly became one of the most popular players ever to don the Red Sox uniform.

Mo will be a welcome addition to the Angels line-up and the Anaheim community.

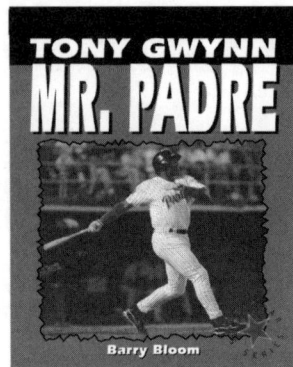

Tony Gwynn:
Mr. Padre

Author: Barry Bloom
ISBN: 1-58261-049-5

Tony is regarded as one of the greatest hitters of all-time. He is one of only three hitters in baseball history to win eight batting titles (the others: Ty Cobb and Honus Wagner).

In 1995 he won the Branch Rickey Award for Community Service by a major leaguer. He is unfailingly humble and always accessible, and he holds the game in deep respect. A throwback to an earlier era, Gwynn makes hitting look effortless, but no one works harder at his craft.

Kevin Brown:
That's Kevin with a "K"

Author: Jacqueline Salman
ISBN: 1-58261-050-9

Kevin was born in McIntyre, Georgia and played college baseball for Georgia Tech. Since then he has become one of baseball's most dominant pitchers and when on top of his game, he is virtually unhittable.

Kevin transformed the Florida Marlins and San Diego Padres into World Series contenders in consecutive seasons, and now he takes his winning attitude and talent to the Los Angeles Dodgers.

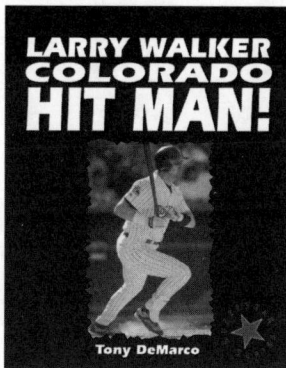

Larry Walker:
Colorado Hit Man!

Author: Tony DeMarco
ISBN: 1-58261-052-5

Growing up in Canada, Larry had his sights set on being a hockey player. He was a skater, not a slugger, but when a junior league hockey coach left him off the team in favor of his nephew, it was hockey's loss and baseball's gain.

Although the Rockies' star is known mostly for his hitting, he has won three Gold Glove awards, and has worked hard to turn himself into a complete, all-around ballplayer. Larry became the first Canadian to win the MVP award.

Sandy and Roberto Alomar: Baseball Brothers

Author: Barry Bloom
ISBN: 1-58261-054-1

Sandy and Roberto Alomar are not just famous baseball brothers they are also famous baseball sons. Sandy Alomar, Sr. played in the major leagues fourteen seasons and later went into management. His two baseball sons have made names for themselves and have appeared in multiple All-Star games.

With Roberto joining Sandy in Cleveland, the Indians look to be a front-running contender in the American League Central.

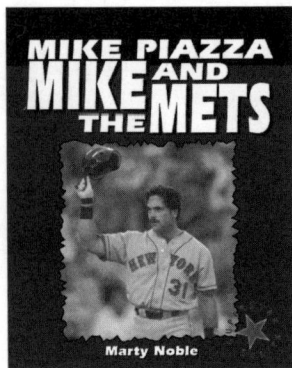

Mike Piazza: Mike and the Mets

Author: Marty Noble
ISBN: 1-58261-051-7

A total of 1,389 players were selected ahead of Mike Piazza in the 1988 draft, who wasn't picked until the 62nd round, and then only because Tommy Lasorda urged the Dodgers to take him as a favor to his friend Vince Piazza, Mike's father.

Named in the same breath with great catchers of another era like Bench, Dickey and Berra, Mike has proved the validity of his father's constant reminder "If you work hard, dreams do come true."

Curt Schilling: Phillie Phire!

Author: Paul Hagen
ISBN: 1-58261-055-x

Born in Anchorage, Alaska, Schilling has found a warm reception from the Philadelphia Phillies faithful. He has amassed 300+ strikeouts in the past two seasons and even holds the National League record for most strikeouts by a right handed pitcher at 319.

This book tells of the difficulties Curt faced being traded several times as a young player, and how he has been able to deal with off-the-field problems.

Mark McGwire: Mac Attack!

Author: Rob Rains
ISBN: 1-58261-004-5

Mac Attack! describes how McGwire overcame poor eyesight and various injuries to become one of the most revered hitters in baseball today. He quickly has become a legendary figure in St. Louis, the home to baseball legends such as Stan Musial, Lou Brock, Bob Gibson, Red Schoendienst and Ozzie Smith. McGwire thought about being a police officer growing up, but he hit a home run in his first Little League at-bat and the rest is history.

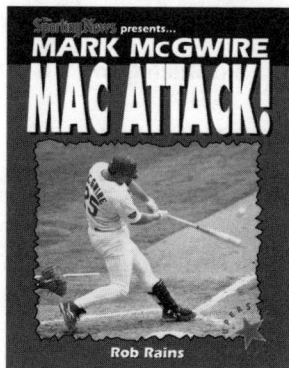

Roger Clemens: Rocket Man!

Author: Kevin Kernan
ISBN: 1-58261-128-9

Alex Rodriguez: A-plus Shortstop

ISBN: 1-58261-104-1

Baseball
SuperStar Series Titles

____ Sandy and Roberto Alomar: Baseball Brothers

____ Kevin Brown: Kevin with a "K"

____ Roger Clemens: Rocket Man!

____ Juan Gonzalez: Juan Gone!

____ Mark Grace: Winning With Grace

____ Ken Griffey, Jr.: The Home Run Kid

____ Tony Gwynn: Mr. Padre

____ Derek Jeter: The Yankee Kid

____ Randy Johnson: Arizona Heat!

____ Pedro Martinez: Throwing Strikes

____ Mike Piazza: Mike and the Mets

____ Alex Rodriguez: A-plus Shortstop

____ Curt Schilling: Philly Phire!

____ Sammy Sosa: Slammin' Sammy

____ Mo Vaughn: Angel on a Mission

____ Omar Vizquel: The Man with a Golden Glove

____ Larry Walker: Colorado Hit Man!

____ Bernie Williams: Quiet Superstar

____ Mark McGwire: Mac Attack!

SP
SPORTS
PUBLISHING
INC.

Available by calling 877-424-BOOK